Susan McCune

New York

Alyssa cannot believe she is at space camp! She has been looking forward to it for weeks.

Alyssa meets her counselor. She meets the other campers, too. Alyssa cannot wait to learn all about space.

They learn about rockets and what astronauts do. They learn about the first mission to the moon.

The next day, they go in a special
machine. There are special machines
that astronauts use to train for space.
It makes them feel like they are really
in space!

They learn about gravity. They learn
that in space there is less gravity than
there is on Earth. They sit in a special
chair. It lets them feel what it is like
to float.

They look at real control panels for a
space shuttle. There are a lot of screens
and special buttons.

Alyssa and the other campers learn about the International Space Station. It is a satellite where astronauts can stay. They do experiments and run tests.

The campers talk to the astronauts at the space station. They talk to them using a web camera.

Students planted sunflower seeds. A tray of seedlings went up to the International Space Station. Scientists want to learn how plants grow in space. The campers see the sunflowers growing.

It is the day before camp ends. Alyssa sits in a machine that spins around in all directions. It feels like a spacecraft tumbling through space.

Alyssa's parents come to pick her up. She tells them all about space camp on the ride home. She learned a lot!